CW00855102

MONA
the
Champion

MONA
the
Champion

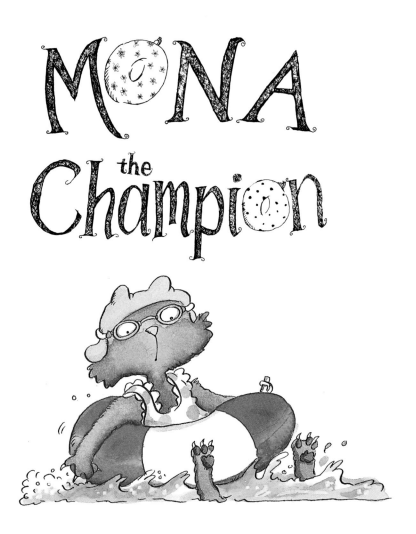

Sonia Holleyman

ORCHARD BOOKS

For Matthew

ORCHARD BOOKS
96 Leonard Street, London EC2A 4RH
Orchard Books Australia
14 Mars Road, Lane Cove, NSW 2066
ISBN 1 85213 549 2 (hardback)
ISBN 1 85213 670 7 (paperback)
First published in Great Britain 1993
First paperback publication 1995
© Sonia Holleyman 1993
The right of Sonia Holleyman to be identified as the author of
this work has been asserted by her in accordance with the
Copyright, Designs and Patents Act, 1988.
A CIP catalogue record for this book is available from the British Library.
Printed in Belgium

One sunny Saturday morning Mona and
her Dad arrived at the swimming pool. Mona
knew that today was going to be brilliant
because her cat, Fang, was having his first
swimming lesson.

Fang was hiding inside Mona's sports bag.
"Cats aren't allowed!" Mona whispered.

"One child and one spectator, please," Dad said, when they reached the counter. They took their tickets and Mona carried her sports bag into the changing rooms.

"Have fun," said Dad.

Mona had her swimming costume on under
her clothes, but she helped Fang into his, and
tucked in his tail.

"You'll have no need to worry," said Mona.
"I'm a champion swimmer." And she showed
Fang her badges. One of them proved she
could swim a whole length underwater.

"Maybe you'll win a badge too," said Mona,
as she and Fang made their way to the pool.
Fang couldn't believe his eyes. He had never
seen so much water!

A swimming gala was in full swing.
Coloured floats separated the part of the pool
which was being used for the competition.
The swimmers dived in at the deep end and
raced down the lanes.

"The winner gets a medal," said Mona
enviously.

Then she fixed her goggles over her eyes and leapt into the pool with a shriek.

Fang didn't want to get water up his nose,
so he carefully climbed down the ladder. The
water was cold and much too wet. He was
sure he was going to sink.

"Floating is the first thing to learn," said Mona as she splashed up to him. "Then you must kick your legs and dig with your front paws. This is called the doggy paddle."

Dad looked up from his paper. He was glad
Mona had found a nice little friend to play with.

Fang splashed and kicked out his back legs and clawed the water with his front paws. The trouble was, things just got in the way. But Mona was impressed.

"Now I'll teach you to swim underwater."
She pulled a mask and snorkel over Fang's
head and poked his feet into a pair of flippers.
   "Brilliant!" cried Mona, as Fang bubbled
under.

Fang blinked. He couldn't see any fishes: only knees, toes and bottoms. With a swish of his flippers, he slowly sank to the bottom of the pool.

Mona watched Fang proudly then she put on her special plastic shark's fin.

"This is going to be the best trick ever!" she thought as she dived underwater.

Mona prowled up and down the pool, with her shark's fin cutting through the water. It was easy to surprise the swimmers as she appeared beside them.

"There's a shark in the water!" they cried,
rushing to the edge of the pool and up the
ladders to escape.

Meanwhile, Fang paddled along underwater, trying to hold his breath and puff the water from his snorkel. Water bubbled up his nose and into his ears. He couldn't see where he was going.

But Mona was having a brilliant time.
"There is *so* much room," she thought as she
swam upside down. "Where is everyone?"

Dad looked up. The pool seemed much emptier, even in the special gala lanes. There was just one competitor – and he seemed to be winning.

The swimmers huddled around on the edge of the pool trying to catch a glimpse of the dangerous creature splashing around in the foaming water.

The pool attendant arrived with a net.

Fang paddled furiously. He was beginning
to fancy himself as a catfish. But it was hard
work, this doggy paddle, and his paws were
getting tired. He paddled a bit harder and
grabbed hold of the nearest edge.

"Congratulations," cried the judge as he took Fang by the paw. "You were the only swimmer to enter the final!"

Dad cheered. He was glad Mona's new friend had won the race. But where was Mona?

Then his eyes fell on the crowd of swimmers at the pool's edge and he watched with everyone as the lifeguard dipped his net into the water and chased the shark around the shallow end.

"I don't believe it!" Dad groaned, as Mona was carried, wriggling, to the poolside. "I have never been so shocked."

But he was really mad when he found a soggy Fang beneath the swimming hat. Fang had to return his winner's medal *immediately*.

"Well, I thought it was a good joke," Mona told Fang, as they had their showers. "But now we've been banned from the pool and Dad is in a mean mood!"

Fang was just glad his swimming lesson
was over. He could still feel the water bubbling
up his nose.

They found Dad waiting for them outside.
"It's time you found a nice hobby that will
keep you out of trouble," he told Mona crossly.

Mona and Fang were packed into the back
of the car and Dad started the drive home.
"I didn't really mean to cause trouble,"
Mona said, as she rummaged in her sports
bag. "But you must agree," she said proudly,
"that Fang is a brilliant swimmer."

And with that Mona handed over Fang's special award. Dad smiled as Fang took his own underwater badge and agreed. Fang was a champion swimmer.